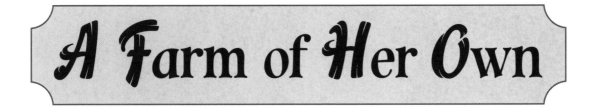

A Farm of Her Own

A Farm of Her Own

Natalie Kinsey-Warnock

illustrated by Kathleen Kolb

DUTTON CHILDREN'S BOOKS

NEW YORK

In loving memory of Aunt Ada and Uncle Will
and their daughter, Marion   N.K.W.

To my dear, darling daughter and son, Anna and Nathan,
and with fond memories of Sandra Miaow-mo Kitty Cat
                                                K.K.

Text copyright © 2001 by Natalie Kinsey-Warnock

Illustrations copyright © 2001 by Kathleen Kolb

All rights reserved.

CIP Data is available.

Published in the United States 2001 by Dutton Children's Books,

a division of Penguin Putnam Books for Young Readers

345 Hudson Street, New York, New York 10014

www.penguinputnam.com

Designed by Alan Carr • First Edition

Printed in Hong Kong • ISBN 0-525-46507-3

1   3   5   7   9   10   8   6   4   2

AUTHOR'S NOTE

Will and Ada Drew Urie were both born in Glover, Vermont—Will on a farm and Ada in a logging camp—but Ada's family soon moved to her grandfather's farm. When Will and Ada married, they moved to a farm of their own and worked side by side for the next sixty years—haying, milking, maple sugaring, cutting wood, and raising five children. They never owned a tractor, preferring to do all the farmwork by hand or by horse-power. Ada always claimed she wouldn't be happy unless she had her hands in the soil. She tended to her vegetable gardens and orchard and was known for her berry picking, her beautiful flowers, and her baked goods. I especially miss her doughnuts.

Will and Ada were my great-uncle and great-aunt. This book is for them.

Natalie Ada Kinsey-Warnock

*E*mma had never milked a cow. She had never gathered eggs or ridden a horse, either. But all that changed when she was ten years old.

Emma's family lived in a small apartment over the bank in Barton. Mama and Papa both worked in the furniture mill. They were working long hours to save enough money for a house of their own. So Emma was going to spend the summer with her great-aunt Ada and great-uncle Will at Sunnyside Farm.

Aunt Ada and Uncle Will made Emma think of birds. Uncle Will was tall and gawky like a heron, while Aunt Ada was small and quick and cheerful as a wren. Aunt Ada said the old farm wasn't much to look at when they first bought it. The house had stood empty for thirty-nine years, but she and Uncle Will had hammered and plastered and painted and papered and had turned it into a home.

Emma didn't know if she'd like Sunnyside Farm, but as summer went on, she didn't want to leave.

All her favorite sounds
were on that farm—
    cowbells and bullfrogs
    and rain on the roof,
and her favorite smells, too—
    wild roses
    and horses
    and homemade bread.

It was a busy farm,
     with haying and milking
     and weeding,
     and cows and calves
     and chickens and lambs to be fed—
so much work it seemed
there could never be time for fun.
But there was.

At first Emma was shy with her cousins,

Edwin and Earl, Lucy and Pearl,

but soon she was climbing apple trees,

jumping in the hay,

and swimming in the pond,

and it was as if she'd known them all her life.

Emma loved caring for the animals, too:
>   dark-eyed calves she taught to drink from a pail,
>   new kittens in the haymow,
>   and Jack, a white horse Uncle Will
>   had bought years before
>   "for a song," he said.

No one knew how old Jack was. He was so tall that Emma and her cousins had to climb the rail fence to get on his back, but he was gentle and nuzzled Emma when she brought him apples and sugar.

When the hay was ready to cut, Uncle Will rode the McCormick mower behind old Jack, and the blade sang *clack, clack, clack*. Later, Uncle Will raked the hay into long windrows. When the hay was dry, he pitched it, loose, up into the wagon, while Emma and her cousins trampled it down. Just when they were so hot and thirsty they couldn't stand it one more minute, they'd see Aunt Ada coming across the field, swinging a jug of ice-cold lemonade for them to drink in the shade.

Sometimes, if there weren't storm clouds hurrying him along, Uncle Will told them stories—

    of wildcats
    and bears
    and Great-Grandfather's
    journey from Scotland.

Aunt Ada told stories, too—
    of being born in a blizzard,
    Uncle Will coming to court her in his shiny
        buggy pulled by a high-stepping horse,
    and helping her father dig potatoes one
        September snowstorm.
"I always wanted to be a farmer," she said.

"Not me," said Pearl. "I'm going to be a doctor."

Edwin wanted to be a scientist, Earl a carpenter, and
  Lucy a teacher.

"And what about you, Emma?" Aunt Ada asked.

"I want to be a farmer—like you," Emma said shyly.

Her cousins laughed, but Aunt Ada just smiled.

"It's hard work, but it's been a happy life for me,"
  she said, rubbing her rough hands.

It was those hands Emma would always remember,
    hands that gathered eggs
    and shelled peas
    and made warm, golden doughnuts,
    and her strong arms that raked hay
    and churned butter
    and could hug five children at once.
Aunt Ada loved gardening.
She grew flowers and vegetables
and filled her pantry shelves

with jars of preserves all lined up in rows—
corn and carrots,
tomatoes and beans,
and berries of all kinds—
raspberries and blueberries,
gooseberries and currants—
for cobblers and pies
and jams and jellies
that sparkled like jewels
and won blue ribbons at the county fair.

Sometimes, after supper
and games of hide-and-seek under a starry sky,
Uncle Will would call out, "Who wants to make ice cream?"
Edwin and Earl would run to the icehouse
   for a block of ice.
Aunt Ada would cook a custard
      of cream, sugar, eggs, and vanilla,
      and add wild strawberries, too.
She'd pour it into the ice-cream freezer,
surrounded by ice chips and salt,
and they'd all take turns cranking the freezer
and licking the dasher.

Emma loved those nights most,
      all of them gathered on the porch steps,
      while bullfrogs sang from the pond
      and fireflies danced in the yard.

September came, and Emma went back to school
and the small apartment in Barton.
She was happy to see Mama and Papa,
but she missed Aunt Ada and Uncle Will,
her cousins, and Jack.

Whenever she remembered Sunnyside Farm,
pictures came to her mind, pictures she knew she'd
never forget—
        of fields painted with daisies and buttercups,
        blue vetch and clover,
        of Aunt Ada humming in her garden,
        and starry nights as restful as sleep.

Uncle Will died when he was ninety-three,
and Aunt Ada cared for the farm as best she could.
But then she died, too.

Emma went on to college and got married.
She kept in touch with her cousins,
but she didn't drive by Sunnyside Farm anymore.

Someone else lived there now.
Someone who didn't care about hay rakes or cookstoves
or Jack's old harness, and he parked his truck
where Aunt Ada's flower garden used to be.

Emma told her children stories about
Aunt Ada and Uncle Will
and only dreamed of a farm of her own,
until her cousin Lucy called one day
to tell her Sunnyside Farm was for sale again.

Emma lives there now,

    with cows and lambs

    and an old horse named Jack

    (though not the same one, of course).

The house had gotten run down,

but Emma and her husband, Frank, papered

and painted and turned it into a home again.

Her cousins' children visit and play

with her children.

    They climb apple trees,

    jump in the hay,

    and swim in the pond,

and it's as if they've known each other,

and that farm, all their lives.

Some days, when Emma is in the fields,
she can almost hear the *clack, clack, clack* of the mower,
and sometimes, in the garden, if she closes her eyes,
she sees Aunt Ada there, too,
and hears her sweet laughter ring like birdsong.